A Gift of a Goat

Written and Illustrated by

Eastern Elementary Students

Pleasureville, Ky.

Edited by Robin Tillman

HEIFER®
INTERNATIONAL

"Heifer International is a nonprofit organization working to end hunger and poverty while caring for the Earth. For more than 70 years, we have provided livestock and environmentally sound agricultural training to improve the lives of those who struggle daily for reliable sources of food and income. Together, we have power over poverty."

This beautiful story was written as a cumulative poem by students at Eastern Elementary School in Pleasureville, Ky. The kindergarten, first and second grade students entered and won the Kentucky Association of School Administrators (KASA) Student Impact Grant competition by designing a project based learning unit that would impact a global community. Their project ideas led to the collaborative writing and illustrating of this book.

With the awarded grant money, the students were able to self-publish, "A Gift of a Goat." The money earned from the sale of this book will be used to impact the lives of children and families in West Africa, with the purchase of goats through Heifer International.

I would like to personally thank KASA for the generous grant that made all of this possible and for inspiring my students to impact the world. I would also like to thank Heifer International for providing an avenue through which students can learn and love and give. One goat can change the world.

Robin Tillman

Dedicated to children all over the world.

ESPECIALLY,
MAGGIE,
ELIZA
& RILEY
12-25-21

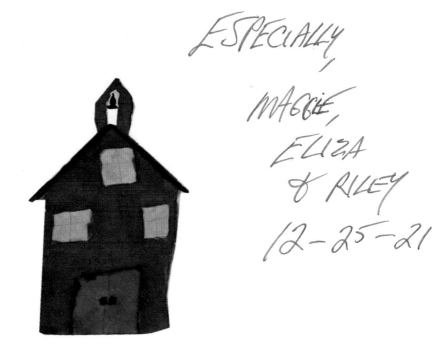

ISBN-10: 1546306072
ISBN-13: 978-1546306078

This is a boy and his goat.

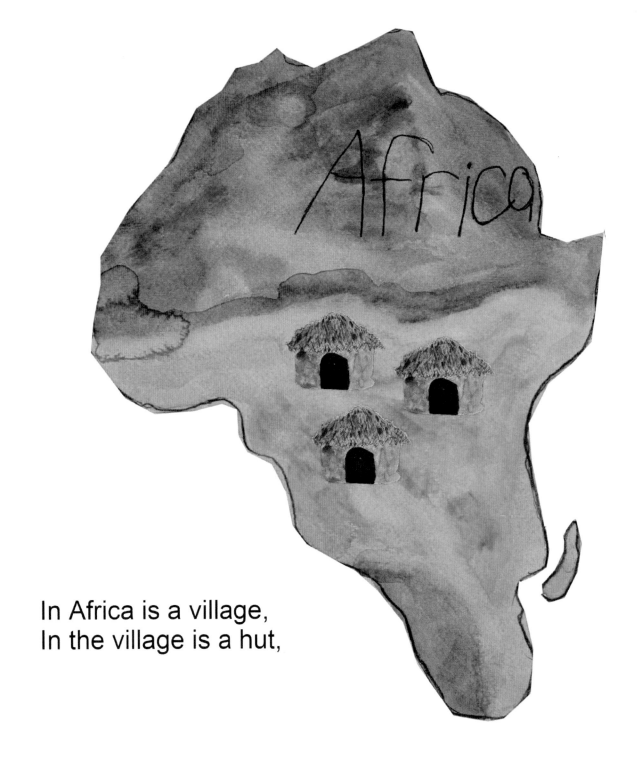

In Africa is a village,
In the village is a hut,

In the hut is a fire,

Near the fire sleeps the boy,

Near the hut sleeps his goat,
A goat named Nunana.
Nunana means gift.

Nunana was a gift for the boy,
A boy named Jabari.

From the goat he gets milk,

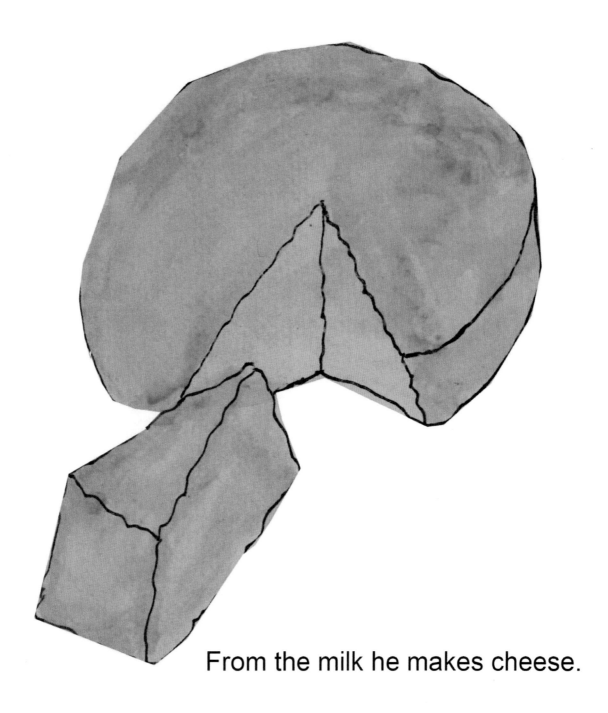

From the milk he makes cheese.

The milk and cheese
make the boy
happy and healthy.

At the market Jabari sells cheese,

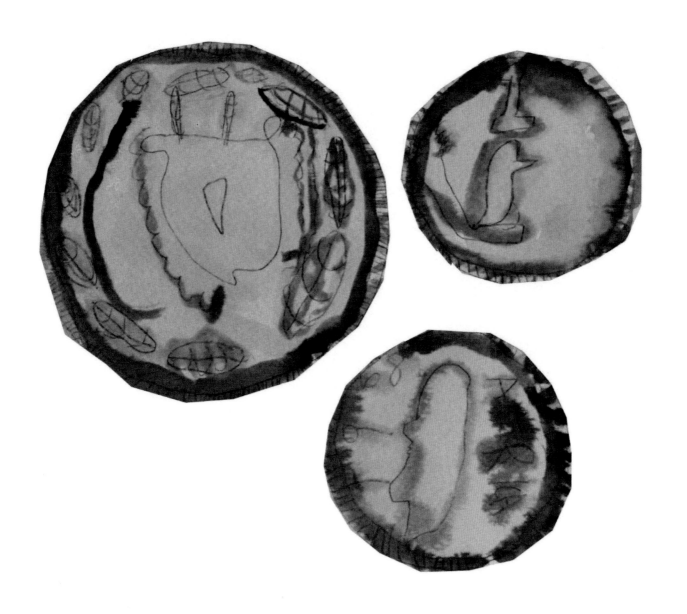

From the cheese he gets coins,

With the coins
he buys shoes,

And pays for school.

Nunana was a gift for the boy,
A boy who drinks milk and eats cheese,

And goes to school.

Jabari loves his gift,

And Nunana loves her boy.

These are the students that worked together to brainstorm ways to impact the world, create a winning KASA grant video, write a thoughtful poem about a child on the other side of the world and illustrate the story with beautiful pictures.

Abigail Adams	Katie Heitzman	Brayden Simpson
Sarah Aldridge	Gavin Hines	Athena Smith
Quentin Armstrong	Kadence Holthouser	Bella Smith
Jacobi Ayers	Nate Hunt	Blane Smith
Danielle Bills	Alexander Kelley	Damien Smith
Jezic Black	Azria Kelley	Dominic Smith
Tristan Breeding	Diamond Kelley	Gabby Smith
Jayden Briscoe	Charles Lancaster	Lena Smith
Nicholas Bryan	Zachary Lancaster	Izabella Snider
Zora Burns	Serenity Lathrem	Jacquelyn Spinks
Joston Butterfield	Liberty Logsdon	Alexis Spurr
Shyenne Carter	Abril Lopez	Quentin Stangle
Bobby Chesser	Angel Lucas	Carrie Stewart
Amber Chisholm	Shawn Lucas	Joshua Stewart
Camden Clubb	Ciara Masters	Keegan Stivers
Marley Cobb	Destiny McCarthy	Eli Suter
Hilary Congleton	Haley McCubbins	Olyvya Sykes-Uriarte
Jason Congleton	Joseph McCubbins	Sabrina Tillman
Trevor Cox	Ariyah McGraw	Alaina Tingle
Jake Crabb	Nicole McLennan	Chase Tuggle
Riley Denny	Brayden Miller	Drake Tuggle
Olivia Drawbaugh	RJ Moody	Andi Underwood
Orlando Escobar	Emmett New	Andrea Villatoro
Hayden Estes	Jayden Nutter	Sophia Walling
Jayce Estes	Emma Oak	Gracie Walls
Samantha Estes	Lyla Oak	Kaleb Walls
Abigail Ethington	Bryson Ott	Wyatt Ward
Ray Finney	Chance Ott	Keeli Webster
Gracey Finney	Jazmine Perez	Alissa Willard
Kylie Ford	Josie Peyton	Isiah Willard
Skylynn Gallentine	Reagan Powell	Alexis Wood
Hailee Gillis	Micah Risky	Braxxtin Woods
Gabriella Gregory	Conner Shaw	Josie Woods
Kayli Hedges	Cooper Shaw	Zayden Zaring
Wyatt Heightchew	Katie Jo Sheehan	
	Tristan Short	